A Lottie Lipton ADVENTURE

The Eagle of Rome

Dan Metcalf

ILLUSTRATED BY
Rachelle Panagarry

MINNEAPOLIS

For Samuel and Hollie Watson

Copyright © Bloomsbury Education 2016
Text copyright © Dan Metcalf
Illustrations © Rachelle Panagarry

This Americanization of *The Eagle of Rome: A Lottie Lipton Adventure* is published by Darby Creek by arrangement with Bloomsbury Publishing Plc.

Darby Creek
A division of Lerner Publishing Group, Inc.
241 First Avenue North
Minneapolis, MN 55401 USA

For reading levels and more information, look up this title at www.lernerbooks.com.

Main body text set in Stempel Schneidler Std Roman 12/24.
Typeface provided by Adobe Systems.

Library of Congress Cataloging-in-Publication Data

Names: Metcalf, Dan, author. | Panagarry, Rachelle, illustrator.
Title: The eagle of Rome : a Lottie Lipton adventure / by Dan Metcalf ; illustrations by Rachelle Panagarry.
Description: Minneapolis : Darby Creek, [2018] | Series: The adventures of Lottie Lipton | "First published 2016 by Bloomsbury Education, an imprint of Bloomsbury Publishing Plc."—Title page verso. | Summary: In 1928, nine-year-old investigator Lottie must find the lost Eagle of Rome and return it to the British Museum before the famous treasure hunter, Lady Viola, finds it and sells the relic to the highest bidder. | Description based on print version record and CIP data provided by publisher; resource not viewed.
Identifiers: LCCN 2016053951 (print) | LCCN 2017013044 (ebook) | ISBN 9781512481938 (eb pdf) | ISBN 9781512481846 (lb : alk. paper) | ISBN 9781512481877 (pb : alk. paper)
Subjects: | CYAC: Antiquities—Fiction. | British Museum—Fiction. | Mystery and detective stories.
Classification: LCC PZ7.1.M485 (ebook) | LCC PZ7.1.M485 Eag 2018 (print) | DDC [Fic]—dc23

LC record available at https://lccn.loc.gov/2016053951

Manufactured in the United States of America
1-43163-32925-3/9/2017

Contents

Chapter One
London, 1928

FLASH!

The camera bulbs popped and fizzled, leaving a stench of soot in the air. Reporters from every major newspaper in the country gathered around the grand entrance to the British Museum, all shouting at once to be heard.

"Over here!"

"Lady Viola!"

"Just one question!"

In front of the crowd of journalists stood a tall woman in her early thirties with short, black, bobbed hair. She wore a khaki shirt and shorts—the kind that would not be out of place on an explorer in a dark jungle. It certainly looked exotic in central London. Peeking out from the front doors behind her, Lottie Lipton stared at the woman, fascinated by her every move.

"Uncle Bert!" called Lottie. "It's so exciting! Imagine, Lady Viola Kirton in *our* museum!"

"Honestly, Lottie dear, I don't see what all

2

the fuss is about. Who exactly *is* this woman?" Uncle Bert harrumphed. He tore open a package that had just arrived for him and found some ancient Roman belt buckles. "Oh, goody! They've

finally come!" Uncle Bert, who was the Curator of Egyptology at the British Museum, had been looking after the Ancient Roman department ever since Cedric, the usual Curator of Roman

Artifacts, had gone on an archaeological dig.

"What?" said Lottie, turning to face her great uncle. "You've never heard of Lady Viola? The famous treasure hunter? The woman who unearthed the Jeweled Skull of Marrakesh? She's in all the newspapers!"

"Ah, I see. I haven't read a paper since 1918, so I must have missed it," said Uncle Bert, still admiring the belt buckles. "However, if she's a trained archaeologist, I very much look forward to meeting her."

Lottie raised her eyebrows and turned

back to Lady Viola and the reporters. She still couldn't believe that Uncle Bert had never heard of Lady Viola! She was one of Lottie's

heroes. She was the daughter of a nobleman and went on daring expeditions to recover lost treasures. Her adventures were always in the papers, and Lottie had cuttings of every story she could find about her. She crept forward to hear what Lady Viola was saying.

"Gentlemen, calm down!" Lady Viola smiled. "I have returned home to my beloved London as I am on the trail of one of the most

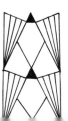

elusive items in history. I hope the British Museum's unique library may contain clues to the whereabouts of"—she paused for dramatic effect—"the Eagle of the Ninth Legion!"

Lottie gasped. She didn't need Uncle Bert to explain what that was! The eagle was the standard (which is a statue used as a symbol) of the legendary lost Ninth Legion—a Roman battalion of ten thousand men who mysteriously went missing when a mist descended on them on the battlefield.

"But that's just a myth!" shouted one of the reporters.

"So was the Crystal Crown of Casablanca before I tracked it down!" said Lady Viola with a wink. The reporters laughed. "Now if you'll excuse me, I have research to do."

Lottie marveled at the way she elegantly turned and walked away from the crowd. *So composed! So charming!* she thought.

"Out of my way, pip-squeak!" said Lady Viola as Lottie rushed to hold the door open for her.

So rude!

Uncle Bert held out his hand to shake Lady Viola's, but she walked past him without even looking.

"Old man, where are the books in this

dump?" she said with a snarl. "I want to get out of here as soon as possible."

Lottie felt crushed. Who was this awful woman? How had she changed from being so polite and charming in front of the reporters to being rude and arrogant?

"I thought this was your 'beloved London'?" said Lottie. Lady Viola let out a laugh.

"Dear me, no! That stuff is just for the papers. They seem to like their heroines plain and polite. London is where I was born, but I don't see why I should be in gray old England when I could be sunning myself in the Mediterranean," said Lady Viola. "Now, books?"

Uncle Bert nodded to Lottie, who reluctantly took the rude lady through the museum to the library. Lottie knew the museum inside out, having lived there since she was four. She and Uncle Bert shared an apartment in the museum. The only other person to live on the grounds of the museum was Reg, the old caretaker, who was currently in the library dusting the bookshelves.

"Ah, this must be Lady Viola!" said Reg, smiling a toothless grin. Lottie tried to stop herself from laughing as he performed a curtsy.

"No time!" said Lady Viola, pushing past him. She marched straight up to the books on ancient Rome and pulled out a heavy volume. "This is the one! I'd prefer not to be here at all, but this is the only copy of this book in existence." She slammed the dusty, old book onto the reading table, pulled in her chair, and held up her hand for silence as she leafed through it. Eventually, she found the page she was looking for. "Aha!"

"What are you going to do with the eagle when you find it?" asked Lottie. "Maybe we could exhibit it here at the museum?"

"Not a chance!" said Lady Viola without looking up. "It's going to be sold to the highest bidder. My vacations don't pay for themselves, you know."

Lottie stamped her foot down.

"B-but you can't!" she shouted. "It's an important piece of history! It belongs in a museum!"

Lady Viola quickly copied down something from the book she had been reading. Then she pushed back her chair, stood up, and leaned down over Lottie so that they were eye to eye, their faces just inches apart.

"Listen, runt," she said. "If you find the treasure, you can do whatever you want with it. *I'm* going to collect the cash."

The rude adventurer flounced out of the library, leaving Lottie and Reg flabbergasted.

"What a little diva!" said Reg. "She should learn some manners!"

Uncle Bert joined them, and Lottie explained what they had just heard.

"Well, I never!" said Uncle Bert, his moustache quivering with rage. "I've half a mind to try and beat her at her own game and find the eagle ourselves."

Lottie grinned.

"Then let's do it! She left the book open at the page she was looking for. Let's see what clue she's following."

Uncle Bert pulled up a chair and sat down to read the old book, which was handwritten in an ornate style. He made several *Hmm's* and *Ahh's*, and then finally:

"Well, well, well! It seems this book

thinks the Eagle of the Ninth Legion is buried somewhere in London. The bad news is, the only clue it gives is this strange little grid."

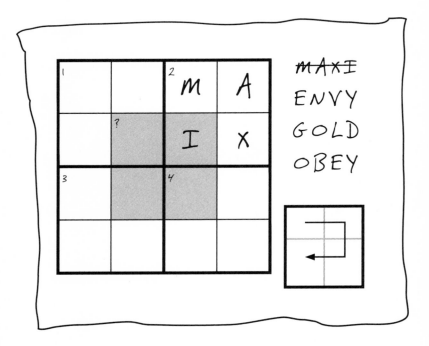

"So . . ." Lottie began to say, leaning over her Uncle's shoulder to look at the book and trying to work out the puzzle. "If we put the words into the numbered boxes so that the word goes clockwise in its square, then we should make a new word in the middle four boxes. Thankfully someone has done the first one for us!" Lottie scratched her head, which was a habit she had picked up from Reg, who was doing the same. She took a deep breath and took out her trusty detective's notebook, which she had filled with useful information and cuttings from newspapers. "All right, then. Let's get cracking!

Can you figure out which words go in the squares? Turn the page to see if you're right!

Ten minutes and several screwed up pieces of notepaper later, Lottie announced she had completed the puzzle with a loud, "Aha!"

"See? The center squares spell out *lion*!"

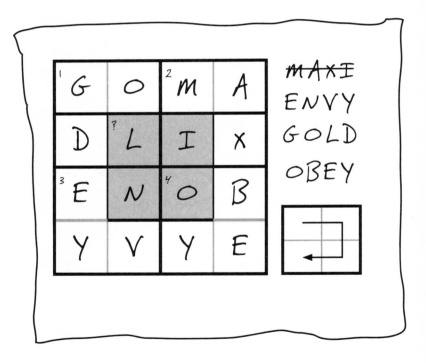

smiled Lottie. "Now what does that mean?"

"The lions in London Zoo?" suggested Reg. Uncle Bert stroked his moustache in thought.

"That's the obvious answer, and probably the one Lady Viola chose," he said. "But what if it was somewhere else . . . somewhere close by . . ."

Lottie pondered until her brain hurt. Just then a pigeon fluttered down outside a nearby window. The sight of the pigeon stirred a memory of when Uncle Bert had taken her to feed the birds in—

"Trafalgar Square!" she blurted out. "There are four giant, bronze statues of lions at the base of Nelson's Column!"

Reg and Uncle Bert exchanged looks and a shrug.

"It's as good a start as any!" said Reg. "I'll start up the car."

Lottie felt the hairs on the back of her neck rise with excitement. She rubbed her hands with glee.

"Lady Viola, we're coming after you!"

Chapter Two

Lottie and Uncle Bert climbed out of the back of Reg's rusty old car after a hair-raising ride.

"Thanks for the lift, Reg," said Lottie, her face white with fear. "I didn't know your car could get up to that speed."

"Me neither!" said Reg, patting the car's steaming hood affectionately.

They stood at the corner of Trafalgar

Square, the grand open area in the center of London. Pigeons fluttered and cooed around them, hoping for a crumb of bread, but Lottie had already eaten her sandwiches. One landed on Reg's shoulder, and he treated it to a small bit of fruitcake that he kept in his pocket for hunger emergencies. In the center of the square stood a giant stone column, standing 170 feet in the air. On top of the column was a statue of Admiral Horatio Nelson.

"Good morning, Admiral!" said Uncle Bert. He was in a jolly mood and saluted the stone sailor. At the base of the column, guarding each corner of the square, were four huge, bronze lions.

"Yikes!" said Reg. "That's a big cat!"

"They're magnificent!" said Lottie, gazing up at the statues. She had always had a soft spot for them. "They were made out of cannons from French ships that were captured by Nelson's fleet. There's an old legend that says the lions will come alive if Big Ben strikes thirteen."

As if she had planned it, she heard a loud sound from down the road.

BONG!

Uncle Bert checked his pocket watch and gulped.

"Twelve o'clock. I hope Big Ben gets its chimes correct!"

Lottie stared down the street to the large

clock tower. She counted the number of bells carefully. She knew that the legend was silly, but stranger things had happened . . .

Two . . . three . . . four . . . five . . .

Lottie counted on her fingers and looked up at the giant claws of the statues.

Six . . . seven . . . eight . . . nine . . .

Reg leaned casually against the wall directly under a huge paw of one of the lions, shaking his head at Lottie and Uncle Bert, who were nearly shaking with nerves.

Ten . . . eleven . . . twelve . . .

And . . . nothing. Silence followed. Lottie breathed easy and laughed.

"I'd say you two were as wacky as brushes, but that would be an insult to brushes!" said Reg. "These cats can't come alive!"

"Strange things seem to happen to us, so I didn't want to take it for granted," said Uncle Bert, putting away his pocket watch, red-faced with embarrassment. Lottie started to walk around the monument.

"Lady Viola doesn't seem to be here," she said.

"One of the security guards said she hailed a taxi and sped off toward London Zoo!" said Reg with a grin. "So we might be ahead of her."

That cheered Lottie up a little, but she still had to find the next clue that would lead them to the eagle.

"So, what exactly *was* the eagle?" pondered Reg as they all began searching for clues.

"Each legion of Roman soldiers had a standard—a kind of small statue on a pole— that they would hold in front of them in battle. It was their symbol, and the Ninth Legion's was a bronze eagle. But it went missing when the legion was curiously lost in a strange mist during a battle," said Uncle Bert.

"So it's not a real eagle then? I wondered why we weren't searching the skies," said Reg. "Why would it be in London?"

Lottie knew this one. "It could be anywhere, but the battle it was lost in was in Scotland, nearly two thousand years ago. Traders and treasure hunters would probably have moved it down to London looking for a buyer."

They continued to search the square, and finally Reg found the next clue. He was standing in front of the lion that faced the National Gallery.

"Is this it?" he called, bringing Uncle Bert and Lottie running over. "I don't know what it means, but it looks kind of clue-like to me."

There were numbers carved into the corners of the paving slabs on the ground directly beneath the lion. It made a large square grid. But the center of the square was missing one paving slab.

Close by, there were some more paving slabs with not only more numbers in the corners, but also with letters in the center.

Main grid (corner numbers of each slab):

8 · 7 / 1 · 5	1 · 3 / 2 · 3	3 · 2 / 2 · 3
3 · 1 / 2 · 3	? ? / ? ?	1 · 1 / 7 · 3
5 · 1 / 9 · 3	2 · 1 / 3 · 3	1 · 2 / 3 · 9

Lettered slabs:

- A: 2 · 5 / 4 · 1
- B: 3 · 5 / 1 · 9
- C: 2 · 4 / 4 · 1
- D: 1 · 6 / 2 · 4

On the platform on which the lion was sitting was carved another message:

$$? = \text{SUM } 10$$

"Math!" said Reg. "Why did it have to be math?"

Lottie scanned the numbers on the ground to see what she had to do.

"It's okay, Reg, I think all we have to do is put a paving slab in the center that makes each of the four numbers in the corners add up to ten."

"That's all very well, but I'll make you a deal—I'll do the lifting if you do the math!"

Lottie tried to block out the sounds of the city around her and concentrate on adding.

Which tile should Lottie choose? Pick one and continue reading to see if you're right.

Lottie bit her lip in concentration as she tried to work out the puzzle. She had worked out that the top left corner of the paving slab she needed to pick should have a two on it, but it didn't help as lots of the spare paving slabs around the puzzle had twos in the top left corner!

"Come on, Lottie!" said Uncle Bert. "It's only a matter of time before Lady Viola realizes her mistake and works her way back here."

"I'm trying!" said Lottie. Eventually she settled on the tile marked with a C, which she thought was correct. Reg pulled out a small crowbar that he kept in his overalls for just such an emergency. He was amazingly strong for his age and lifted the paving slab in one go while Uncle Bert kept watch. They didn't want any policemen to come and ask why they were pulling up the tiles in the center of London!

"Here we go then!" Reg grunted as he shifted the slab into place.

For a moment, nothing happened.

Then:

ROOOAAAAR!

They jumped back as the lion in front of them let out a cry. Its metal mouth opened to reveal a deep, dark hole inside. Lottie smiled as she realized

that the lion wasn't alive—it was mechanical!
Its jaw was designed to open wide enough for a
person to crawl into, and the roar that she had
heard was simply the grinding
of metal.

"Crikey!" cried Reg.

"I think my heart just skipped a beat!"

Lottie rolled up her sleeves and started to climb up the platform to reach the lion's mouth.

"What on Earth are you doing?" asked Uncle Bert, mopping his sweating brow with a handkerchief.

"The eagle is close by, I can feel it!" said Lottie as she reached the lion's fangs. "And I'm not going to let Lady Viola sell it off like a simple trinket. Come on!"

Chapter Three

Inside the lion was dark and dusty. Lottie, being only nine years old, fit through the lion's mouth easily. She slid down a short tunnel that took her underneath the base of Nelson's Column. For Reg and Uncle Bert, however, it was a bit of a squeeze.

"Push!" called Uncle Bert. Outside, Reg was pushing Uncle Bert's large bottom into the

mouth of the lion and getting a few strange
looks from passing Londoners.

"I'm trying!" shouted Reg. "That's it! No
more cakes for you!" He took a few steps
back and then ran up to the professor's

behind and gave one last large shove. It did the trick, and Uncle Bert yelped as he whizzed through the short passage.

He ended up on his back looking up at Lottie.

"Tell me again why we're putting ourselves through this?" he muttered, picking himself up and brushing the dust off his suit.

"For the sake of history and archaeology," said Lottie. She turned to look around and found that they were underneath the column itself, but instead of tons of rock and brick, she found that the space was open, like a giant cavern propped up with sturdy brick beams. The ground they were standing on was made up of large stone tombs.

"Goodness gracious!" gasped Uncle Bert. "A Roman burial ground! The builders of

Nelson's Column must have preserved it when they dug out the foundations! *Oof!*"

Reg slid down the tunnel and bashed into Uncle Bert, so they both ended up back on the

floor. Lottie left them to bicker as she walked through the ancient cemetery. Light came from tiny chinks in the roof above, where the stones didn't join together. The midday sun peeking through meant that Lottie was able to make out quite a few of the inscriptions on the tombs.

"I can't read this one," she said aloud. Uncle Bert stopped his bickering, pulled himself off the ground, and came over to inspect the carved stone.

"It's in Latin. I'll have to get you familiarized with the basic verbs and grammar when we get back to the museum," said Uncle Bert. Lottie groaned—*more* homework! "These must have been here for two thousand years, ever since

38

the Romans called the settlement *Londinium*."

"Wow!" said Lottie. "Has London really been around since Roman times?"

"Even longer," said Uncle Bert. He polished his glasses so he could see the inscription better. "Before the Romans arrived, there was a tribe of Britons that lived here. They called it *Llon dyn*, which means 'ship hill.' The Romans thought it was a good place for a fort, and so they built the settlement up into the biggest Roman town in the country. It even had a large port and an amphitheater where you could watch gladiators fight each other."

"Ugh!" said Lottie. "That's horrible!"

Reg had wandered all the way over to the far side of the burial ground and was furiously rubbing at a door that he had found. He just couldn't help himself when it came to cleaning. It was an ornate design, and there were Roman columns on each side of it, which had been carved from white marble.

"This ain't Latin," Reg called over. "I don't know *what* it is."

They joined the caretaker and puzzled over the markings on the wall.

"You're in top form today, Reg," said Lottie. "I think you've found the next clue!"

Reg grinned and took a bow.

"I find 'em, you solve 'em!"

Lottie could see that the markings on the door were in a grid. Inside each square were symbols that she recognized, but couldn't quite work out.

I				V	
	IV	V		I	
V		I	II	III	
	I	IV	III	VI	
IV			V	II	
	V				III

"Where have I seen these before?" she muttered to herself. Then she remembered. "That's it! The library at the museum has lots of books with these markings. They're Roman numerals!" She hastily pulled out her detective's notebook. She flipped through the pages until she found the right one.

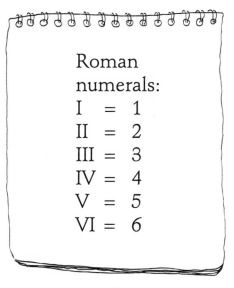

Roman
numerals:
I   =   1
II =   2
III =   3
IV =   4
V   =   5
VI =   6

"Romans didn't use the numbers we use," Lottie explained to Reg. "They used 'I' for one, then 'II' for two, and so on."

Uncle Bert looked down at the ground and found lots of tiles with Roman numerals lying on the floor.

"It looks as though we need to complete the grid," he said. "Every line that goes up and down must have the numbers one through six in it. Also, the smaller boxes must have the numbers one through six in them too, and it looks as though you can't repeat numbers. I suppose these tiles slide in to the empty spaces, which then opens the door."

Reg scratched his head.

"You lost me at numerals."

Lottie was almost breathless with excitement. Behind that door could be the lost Eagle of the Ninth Legion! She tried to concentrate and complete the puzzle in front of her.

Can you put the right numerals in the empty spaces? Continue reading to have a go.

Lottie placed the tiles into the spaces on the grid. Uncle Bert tried to help but kept making mistakes, so Lottie soon gave him the job of handing her the tiles.

"Four, please," she said. "That's 'IV.'"

"I know!" said Uncle Bert, getting muddled with his fours and sixes. Soon they had just one square left. Lottie's heart was pounding a drumbeat on her ribcage. She placed the last square in the space to complete the grid:

I	II	III	IV	V	VI
III	IV	V	VI	I	II
V	VI	I	II	III	IV
II	I	IV	III	VI	V
IV	III	VI	V	II	I
VI	V	II	I	IV	III

There was a moment of silence, interrupted only by the passing rumble of a bus on the road above their heads. Then there was a series of clicks and clunks—the door had unlocked!

"Here we go!" said Lottie as she pulled open the ancient door.

Chapter Four

By the power of Jupiter!" exclaimed Uncle Bert.

"Jeepers!" cried Lottie.

"Bloomin' 'eck!" said Reg.

The three stood on a ledge in a cave. The ledge looked out over a sheer drop to some sharp rocks below them. A fall or slip would send them tumbling to their peril! Lottie gulped with nerves. She wanted to step back into the burial site, but something on the other side of the cave caught her eye. A glint of metal, shining in the darkness.

"The eagle!" she whispered as she pointed to where it lay.

Reg and Uncle Bert squinted in the direction Lottie was pointing and could make out the outline of the eagle, its proud

beak looking as

shiny as ever.

Light shone down like spotlights through miniscule cracks in the cave roof. This illuminated the ledge they were on, but also cast some light to reveal the floor in front of them—one that connected the ledge they were on to the other side of the cave where the eagle lay. Laid out on hexagonal tiles were letters. There did not seem to be a pattern to them, but Lottie knew that this must be her next task.

Uncle Bert leaned against the wall of the cave and felt something cold on his back. He turned to see a plaque on the wall with a message written on it in Latin. He peered at it and began to translate it.

"How much would you be willing to bet that if I stepped on the wrong tile, I'd fall down to the spiky rocks below?" said Lottie. She had been in scrapes before where a booby-trapped puzzle could mean getting seriously hurt, so she wasn't about to take any chances.

"Oh, I'd be willing to bet your life . . ."

The voice came from behind them, making them all jump. They turned to see the pristine black bob of Lady Viola Kirton. She smiled at them like a snake choosing which mouse to eat first.

"How on Earth did you find us?" asked Uncle Bert. Lady Viola strolled along the ledge, looking over to the eagle and licking her lips.

"Once I had exhausted the red herring of London Zoo, I naturally came to Trafalgar Square, where a bronze lion with its mouth gaping open had attracted some attention. I must say, I hadn't expected to see your little group here. You should leave treasure hunting to the experts, you know."

Lottie bristled with anger.

"We *are* the experts!" she shouted. "We

weren't going to let you get the eagle and sell it. It would just sit in a house somewhere, where no one could see it. It should be in a museum. *Our* museum!"

Lady Viola let out a long laugh that echoed around the cave.

"You've got spirit, little one!" she said. "But I've got experience. How were you planning to get across this little path?"

Uncle Bert stepped in between Lady Viola and Lottie.

"We would use our brains, of course," he said. "Anyway, I've just found this plaque on the wall. It will tell us exactly what to do."

"Uncle Bert! Don't tell her what to do!"

Uncle Bert looked flustered as he realized he had let their competition in on their secret.

"Don't worry, it's in Latin, which I doubt she has bothered to learn."

Lady Viola took one glance at the plaque and translated it instantly.

"All hail Gaius, Father of his Country, the true Emperor," she said. "Hmm, there's only one Emperor I know of called Gaius . . ."

She stepped forward to walk on the tiles, placing her boot on one with a *J* on it. She looked shocked when it crumbled underneath her. She wobbled slightly but managed to fall backward onto the ledge.

"Lottie, quick!" said Uncle Bert. "The answer is Julius Caesar! You must step on the right letters, but you can't jump over any. One slip would mean the end. Pick only the tiles that directly join onto the one you are standing on. Go!"

Lottie knew she had to beat Lady Viola across the cave, but she had to pick the right path. She held her breath and stood on her first tile . . .

Can you help
Lottie get to the eagle?
Remember that you can only
pick the tiles that join up
directly and the letters must
spell out JULIUS CAESAR. Good
luck! See if you picked
the right path by turning
the page.

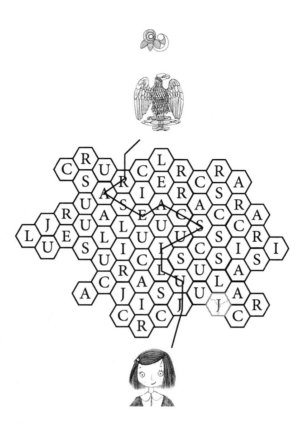

Step by step, Lottie picked her tiles carefully, knowing each time she placed her foot down, it could crumble underneath her. Lady Viola followed her, hopping from one tile to another.

Some crumbled underneath her, but she always managed to save herself from falling to the rocks below. Lottie neared the eagle and realized she had done it!

She grabbed the eagle and held it close to her. It was heavy and seemed to shine with light, as though it was pleased that it was Lottie who had picked it up, not Lady Viola. Lottie felt proud that she had gotten it, but there was no time to celebrate as Lady Viola was on her tail! Lottie heard a creak and the sound of stone shifting. She looked up to see a space opening up in the roof of the cave above her. With Lady Viola directly behind her, Lottie had no choice but to climb up the wall of the cave. Still managing to hold the eagle in one hand, she climbed up toward the light of the world above . . .

Chapter Five

Lottie emerged on the far side of Trafalgar Square, popping up from a hole that had opened in the pavement. As she came up, blinking into the light, a crowd of onlookers saw her and came flocking toward her. Two policemen in their blue suits attempted to keep the crowd away.

"'Ello, Miss," said one of the policemen. "What have you got there, then?"

Lottie did not have time to reply before Lady Viola came out of the hole too, red-faced and seething with anger. The crowd recognized her and clapped politely.

"Give me that eagle!" she roared. Her face was curled into a snarl. The crowd, confused at why the normally elegant Lady Viola Kirton was shouting at a little girl and trying to steal her bronze statue, gasped and stopped their applause.

"This belongs to the British people!" said Lottie, hugging the eagle tight. Lady Viola

made a grab for it, but the policeman got in between them. "I found it, and I claim it on behalf of the British Museum," Lottie said.

Reg and Uncle Bert climbed out of the hole and went to protect Lottie. The second policeman had to hold back Lady Viola as she ranted and spat with anger.

"*I'm* the treasure hunter! *I'm* the one who deserves that eagle! You're nothing but a snot-faced, sniveling little *brat*!"

The crowd gasped, and Lottie noticed two reporters at the back, writing down everything Lady Viola was saying.

"Looks like the newspapers will finally get to see the *real* you," Lottie smiled, nodding toward the reporters. Lady Viola looked over at them and screamed.

"Nooooo!" She tried to shake off the policeman holding her, swinging her arms around and punching him in the face. Both policemen jumped on her and began to drag her away to the local police station to calm her down.

"Well done, Lottie dear.

You were very brave," said Uncle Bert. One of the reporters came closer and held up his camera. The three smiled proudly as they held the eagle.

"Ladies and gentlemen," said Lottie to the crowd around them. "Soon to be exhibited at the British Museum for all to see, I proudly present—the lost Eagle of the Ninth Legion!"

The crowd clapped, and Reg pushed Lottie forward to take the applause. She gave a theatrical bow and walked back to the car, the eagle safely in her arms.

Glossary

admiral: a leader of the British Royal Navy

battalion: a large team of soldiers

expedition: a big journey for a special purpose, such as to carry out research

Mediterranean: a large sea in Europe and the countries surrounding it

red herring: a clue that leads someone in the wrong direction

Roman numerals: the system of writing down numbers in ancient Roman times

standard: a large pole with a flag or ornamental statue on the top, used in battle to show where the leader of the army was

Puzzle

Can you trace a line through the hexagonal tiles, from the bottom to the top, to spell out the name of the rude treasure hunter that Lottie meets in this adventure?

Did You Know?

- The lions that surround Nelson's Column were designed by Edward Landseer in the 1800s, but the lions he studied in London Zoo wouldn't keep still, so the paws are modeled on a cat's!

- Roman numerals are still used today on clock faces, when writing about kings and queens (for example, Henry VIII or Elizabeth II), and when writing the year that a TV program is made.

- The Romans gave us laws, calendars, roads, central heating, and aqueducts that are still used today. Many words in the English language come from Latin.

Conundrum

Can you rearrange these letters to make a different word? A clue has been given for each one to help you!

W	R	A	B	C	O	R

Reg carries one of these in case he needs to open a box or lift a paving slab!

T	O	N	E	B	O	K	O

Lottie carries one of these to write her clues in.

H	I	F	E	N	D	E	R	H	A	C	K

Uncle Bert carries one of these to mop his forehead when he gets hot.

73

Did you manage to solve the clues? Look out for Lottie in her other adventures!

The Catacombs of Chaos

The Curse of the Cairo Cat

The Egyptian Enchantment

The Secrets of the Stone

The Scroll of Alexandria

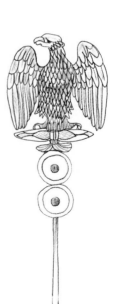